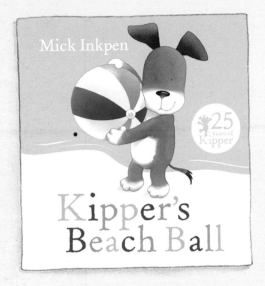

Mick Inkpen

**Kipper's Beach Ball**

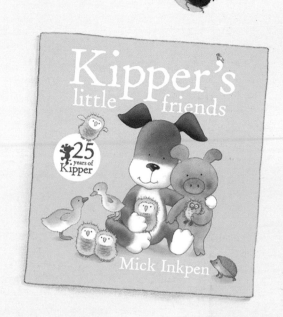

**Kipper's** little friends

Mick Inkpen

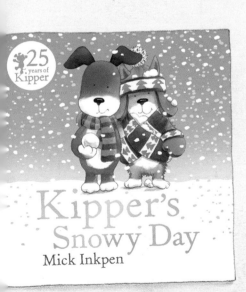

**Kipper's Snowy Day**

Mick Inkpen

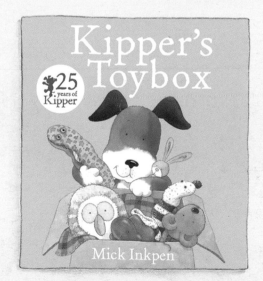

**Kipper's Toybox**

Mick Inkpen

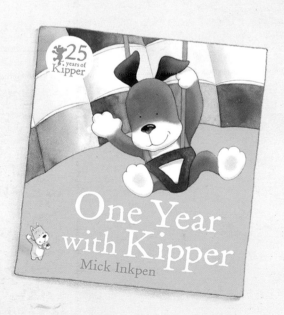

**One Year with Kipper**

Mick Inkpen

What any author wants is for his books to become dog-eared and familiar. I've been lucky enough that my very young readers are particularly adept at giving their books doggy ears in no time at all.

And of all my books, perhaps it's those about Kipper that get the doggiest ears of all, which I guess is kind of appropriate.

*Mick Inkpen*

First published in 1997
by Hodder Children's Books

This edition published in 2015

Text and illustrations copyright © Mick Inkpen 1997

Hodder Children's Books
An imprint of
Hachette Children's Group
Part of Hodder & Stoughton
Carmelite House
50 Victoria Embankment
London EC4Y 0DZ

A catalogue record of this book is available
from the British Library.

ISBN: 978 1 444 92409 1
10 9 8 7 6 5 4 3 2 1

Printed in China

An Hachette UK company
www.hachette.co.uk

# Kipper's Snowy Day

## Mick Inkpen

Hodder
Children's
Books

An imprint of Hachette Children's Group

It was a new morning and it was snowing! Huge cotton wool snowflakes were tumbling past Kipper's window.

'Yes!' said Kipper, jumping out of his basket. 'Yes! Yes!'

He grabbed his scarf and wound it three times round his head. 'Yes! Yes! Yes!'

Kipper was very positive about snow.

Kipper rushed outside.
The snow lay deep and smooth
and new, like an empty page waiting to
be scribbled on. He made a paw print,
and then another.

And then with a whoop he went
charging round and round, criss-crossing
this way and that, until the garden was
full of his tracks.

Kipper stopped to catch his breath, letting the swirling snowflakes melt on his tongue. Then he fell backwards into the snow and lay there panting.

When he stood up he found that he had made a perfect Kipper shaped hole. He tried again. Then he tried a different shape. And another.

'I bet Tiger hasn't thought of this,' he said, and ran off to find his best friend.

Kipper found Tiger at the top of Big Hill. He was wrapped up in a fat bundle of silly, woolly clothes. Kipper plopped a friendly snowball on top of his head.

'Hello,' said Tiger.

Tiger pointed up at the sky. A watery sun was seeping through the grey clouds.

'It won't last,' he said. 'It'll all be gone by tomorrow. There's a warm wind coming.' Tiger was like that. He knew things.

But this was not at all what Kipper wanted to hear, so he started throwing snowballs at his friend.

Tiger was very easy to hit because the silly, woolly clothes were wrapped so tightly around him that he could hardly move. And his own snowballs stuck like little pompoms to the silly, woolly gloves.

'Look at my new game,' said Kipper, falling backwards into the snow. 'You get up very carefully… and there you are!' And there he was, or at least the shape of him.

Tiger stretched out his arms, and fell backwards with a soft, woolly 'crump'. But when he tried to get up he could not. He was too round. He just lay there waving his arms and legs like a beetle on his back.

Tiger heaved himself over onto his tummy, but rolled too far, and found himself on his back again. He tried again. The same thing happened. Snow began to stick in thick lumps to the silly, woolly clothes. Crossly, he heaved himself over once more.

This time he rolled over twice, three times, four times. . .

Slowly at first,
and then a little faster,
and then a lot faster,
and then very fast indeed,
he rolled down the hill.

And as he went the silly,
woolly clothes picked up more and
more snow, so that by the time he
reached the bottom he had changed
from a small dog into a giant snowball.

The giant snowball fell to pieces.

Kipper charged down the hill.
'Are you all right, Tiger?' he panted.
Tiger pulled off his silly, woolly hat.
A big grin spread across his face.
       'Again!' he said.

So that is what they did, all day long, taking turns to wear the silly, woolly clothes.

And by the time the sun began to dip towards the hill making their shadows long and skinny, they had rolled enough snow to the bottom to build a giant snowdog.

They watched their shadows lengthen and fade.

'It'll all be gone by tomorrow,' said Tiger. 'There's a warm wind coming.'

But for once Tiger
was wrong.
The warm wind stayed
away, and that night
another snowstorm smoothed
out all of Kipper's paw prints,
making the garden like a clean,
white, empty page once more.

And the snowdog stood at the
bottom of Big Hill wearing Tiger's
silly, woolly clothes. . .

For almost three. . .                        whole. . .

weeks.

'My children absolutely LOVE all of Mick Inkpen's books, and I still love reading Kipper to them, even when it's for the hundredth time. . .'

Cressida Cowell

'Storytelling at its best.' David Melling

Billy's
Beetle
Mick Inkpen

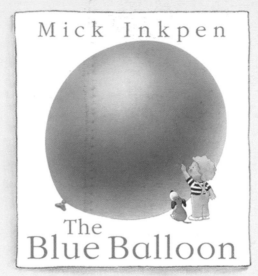

Mick Inkpen

The
Blue Balloon

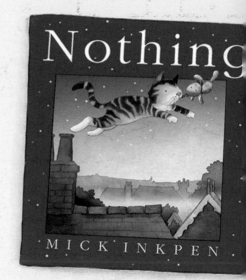

Nothing

MICK INKPEN

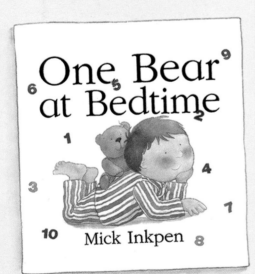

One Bear
at Bedtime
Mick Inkpen

We are
wearing out
the
naughty
step
Mick Inkpen

Threadbear
MICK INKPEN

WITH FOLD-OUT PAGES